THE GHOST THAT BARKED

Read THE WHEELS THAT VANISHED, another **Scooter Spies** mystery!

A Minstrel Book
Available from Pocket Books

Be sure to read Michael Dahl's
Finnegan Zwake mysteries, too!

The Horizontal Man
The Worm Tunnel
The Ruby Raven

Archway Paperbacks
Published by Pocket Books

SCOOTER SPIES Minstrel/December 2000

SCOOTER SPIES

THE GHOST THAT BARKED

MICHAEL DAHL

A MINSTREL® BOOK

Published by POCKET BOOKS

New York   London   Toronto   Sydney   Singapore

A MINSTREL PAPERBACK *Original*

A Minstrel Book published by
POCKET BOOKS, a division of Simon & Schuster, Inc.
1230 Avenue of the Americas, New York, NY 10020

ISBN: 0-7434-1878-6

First Minstrel Books printing December 2000

10 9 8 7 6 5 4 3 2 1

Cover art by Don Stewart

Printed in the U.S.A.

To James "Jimmer" Fairburn
who heard the pointy-eared dog barking

1

BURIED IN THE PIT

Oscar Santiago gazed up at the swirling storm clouds.

DOOO-OOOO-OOOOOM!

Thunder rumbled over the town of Metroville. Oscar felt the aftershocks as they shivered through the tires of his scooter and shook its handlebars. Lightning flashed like a gigantic lightbulb flickering in a gigantic socket. No rain had fallen on the deserted construction site, but Oscar felt the air around him dense with moisture from the nearby Gulf.

"Let's go before the storm hits," he yelled to his friends.

"One more time!" Lily Blue shouted. She balanced on her black-and-gold Stingray scooter at the top of a mountain of loose dirt. Max Martin, his blond hair flashing white in the lightning, stood behind her.

"Go! Go! Go!" urged Max.

Lily's Stingray perched at the end of a wooden

plank that the three of them had found in another corner of the construction site and placed on the dirt as a jumping-off ramp. Lily looked back at Max and smiled. Then she gripped the handlebars of her scooter, lowered her head, and kicked off with all her might. She leaped off the end of the plank and into space.

"YOOOOOOOWWWWEEE!!"

Lily felt the blood race to her head. Wind ripped past her. Lighting flashed and showed the floor of the construction pit rushing up to meet her. With a scream and a grunt she landed at the foot of the mountain in a soft slope of dirt.

"Touchdown!" Lily yelled.

"This place might be a parking ramp next year," said Max. "But for now it's an airstrip!"

The three friends had visited the construction site for the past three nights, after the construction workers had gone home. They took turns flying off the top of the dirt mountain, practicing flips and 360-degree spins. The touchdown site was a smaller mound of dirt at the foot of the mountain. It was the softest spot in the site. With each landing, their scooter tires and sneakers dug deeper and deeper into the soft soil.

Lily hurled herself backward off her black-and-gold Stingray, spread her arms wide, and plopped in the dirt.

"Ouch!"

"What's wrong?" asked Oscar.

Lily looked behind her. "I think I landed on something."

Oscar quickly waved to Max at the top of the mountain. "Don't jump," he yelled. "There's something in the dirt."

Max waved in response and swiftly reversed his scooter, zigzagging down the back side of the mountain. At the bottom he whizzed past stacks of lumber and barrels of paint to reach the landing site on the other side. He pulled his silver scooter alongside Oscar's new electric-blue Vortex Racer.

Oscar had bought the new set of wheels with reward money that the three friends won for uncovering stolen University property. Lily had bought a new terrarium for Speck, her pet chameleon. Speck was awarded a three-month supply of gourmet chameleon food, a tray full of hopping crickets. Max's Hurricane scooter was outfitted with chromium rearview mirrors and a mileage meter. Their united spywork had nabbed a clever thief and solved an impossible disappearance.

"What's in there?" asked Max.

Lily was burrowing in the dirt. "Looks like a box or something," she said.

"A treasure chest!" said Max.

"In the middle of Metroville? There aren't any pirates around here." Oscar looked up at the storm clouds. "Uh-oh, a raindrop."

Max joined Lily, scooping handfuls of dirt away from the buried object.

"They used to be here," said Max. "Pirates, I mean. In the Gulf and Caribbean. My dad told me all about them. Maybe a hundred years ago a pirate ship sailed up the Mixaloopi to bury this stuff."

"Gold coins?" asked Lily.

"Diamonds?" asked Oscar.

"Yeah, which means tickets to the Gulfstream National Scooter Speed-a-thon," said Max.

The three spies scooped with renewed energy. An edge of the trunk angled out of the dirt, its metal corners gleaming like silver in the lightning.

"It *is* a chest!" exclaimed Max.

"It's a cooler," said Oscar.

"No," said Lily, wiping grime from the surface of the trunk. "Look at the fancy painting." The profile of a golden dog with fierce red eyes and pointed ears gleamed on the lid. She traced her finger along golden letters printed below the dog. *Property of Memnon the Magnificent.* "This is an old steamer trunk," she said.

"Pirates sailed on steamships?" asked Oscar.

Lily shook her head. "Not pirates, passengers. People who traveled on big ships like the *Titanic* used these instead of suitcases."

"So this is somebody's underwear?" asked Max.

Oscar laughed. "Yeah, Mr. Memnon's magnificent boxers."

"I think it's locked," said Lily. "Help me pull it all the way out."

The two boys grabbed the thick leather strap on the side of the trunk and tugged. Lily bent her weight and shoved against the side. "Just a . . . little . . . more," she grunted.

Oscar felt a drip again. A raindrop bounced off Lily's head.

Max blinked a bead of water off his lashes. "Here it comes!" he yelled.

Rain struck the construction site like an all-out missile attack. Within seconds, the large mountain of dirt became a melting mound of mud. Muck slid like cool lava into the touchdown site.

"Pull it out!" shouted Lily.

The three spies yanked and pushed the steamer trunk away from the muddy avalanche. Their clothes were dripping wet. Their sneakers sank into the oozy ground. Raindrops beat against the top of the trunk and drummed in their ears.

They dragged the trunk away from the touchdown site and onto a low pile of gravel. "It should be safe here," said Oscar.

Lily's face suddenly went white. "I forgot my scooter!"

She spun around and saw the handlebars of her black-and-gold Stingray slowly sink into a mudhole at the foot of the melting mountain. Lily ran back and waded into the muck. Mud oozed up her

5

thighs. Max and Oscar waded in behind her. She reached out and gripped the handlebars.

"They're stuck," she said.

Oscar and Max each grabbed a handlebar and pulled.

"This is harder than the trunk," grunted Max.

"Better hurry," warned Oscar, pointing up the side of the muddy slope. A thick slice of the mountain, a vast chocolate avalanche, was sliding toward them.

"We'll be buried alive!" shouted Max.

"Not before I find out what's in that trunk," said Lily.

With one terrific pull, they freed the sinking scooter. Lily held it over her head, the mud level with her waist. The three spies held on to each other, slipping and sinking in the muck, as they half-crawled, half-ran back toward the steamer trunk.

When they reached the gravel, Oscar looked behind him. The descending wall of mud had picked up speed, slamming into the touchdown site.

"We could have ended up like the dinosaurs," said Oscar.

"Dang! I lost my shoe!" wailed Max.

"One good thing about this rain," said Lily. "It'll clean the mud off our clothes."

"What about the trunk?" asked Oscar. "We can't leave it here."

Max untied his remaining shoe and peeled off his dripping socks. He squirmed his toes into the wet gravel. "Let's take it to my house," he said.

"What will your dad say?" Lily asked.

"Nothing," replied Max. "We'll hide it in the shed. It's not like we're stealing it. We're investigating, finding out who this Memnon guy is."

"Tomorrow morning, we can try to open it," said Oscar. "Maybe the owner's address is written inside.

"No fair opening it before then," ordered Lily.

Max saluted. "Aye-aye, Captain."

He and Oscar planted the Hurricane and Vortex scooters side by side. The steamer trunk was set lengthwise across the two scooter footboards. Lily laid her Stingray on the steamer's lid and pushed and guided from behind. The boys walked in front of their scooters, dragging the handlebars behind them.

"Mooo!" joked Max.

"*ARRR-OOOOOOOH!*"

The three spies stood still.

"Who's there?" shouted Lily.

The only sound was the rain hitting the ground and drumming against the lid of the trunk.

"Sounded like a dog,"whispered Oscar.

"More like a wolf," added Max.

They scanned the construction site through the wall of pouring rain.

"No dogs," said Oscar.

"Let's get this trunk to your place," said Lily to Max.

As they slipped under the chain hanging across the exit gates, they heard the unearthly howl again.

ARRR-OOOOOOOH!

The boys stopped pulling the handlebars. Lily glanced around quickly. "It sounded like it's right next to us," she said.

"I still don't see any dog around," said Max, squinting into the dark.

"I do," said Oscar.

Lily shivered. "Where?"

Oscar pointed to the lid of the mysterious Memnon's trunk and to the golden profile of the pointy-eared dog.

Lily said to Max, "You still want to hide this in your shed?"

Max snorted. "Don't tell me you guys are afraid of a painting," he said.

ARRR-OOOOOOOH!

"Come on," said Max. " Let's keep moving. I think my dad bought a new padlock for the shed door."

2

BLUE PRINTS

"Did you hear that dog barking in the middle of the night?" asked Dylan Martin.

Max stared across the breakfast table at his older brother. Dylan was chomping on peanut butter toast.

"Dog?" said Max. "What dog?"

"How should I know?" said Dylan. "Some dumb dog woke me up after midnight. And I couldn't get back to sleep. Now I'll be no good at soccer practice."

Mr. Martin entered the kitchen, his nose buried in a thick textbook. "What's this about getting a dog?" he said.

"Why are you up so early, Dad?" asked Dylan, shoving more bread slices into the toaster. "You should sleep late. School's out."

"Only for another week," said Mr. Martin. "And Dylan, what did I tell you about not wearing sunglasses inside the house?"

Mr. Martin poured himself a glass of orange

juice without looking at either the glass or the orange pitcher. He sat down at the table, still reading. Suddenly he looked up, set his book in his lap, and squinted out the window. "Did either of you boys hear a dog barking last night?"

Max had heard the dog barking. It was the same howl he and Oscar and Lily had heard echoing in the construction site last night. An eerie wolflike cry that pierced his bedroom walls long after midnight. Like his brother, Max also hadn't been able to sleep.

After breakfast, Dylan zipped off on his motorcycle for soccer practice and Mr. Martin walked into his office. Max ran outside to check the steamer trunk hidden in the shed. Gray rainclouds hung overhead. A few streetlights glowed in the gloomy morning.

"Weird," said Max. "Looks like time to go to bed, not get up."

The Martins had no garage. The car and motorcycle parked on a brick driveway next to the house. A brick path led from the driveway to the shed at the backyard.

Max unlocked the door with the shed key he had slipped into his jeans last night. He breathed a sigh of relief. The steamer trunk was still there. It sat in the far corner, hidden beneath a green plastic tarp.

As he turned to leave, Max looked down. A pair of blue footprints glowed at the edge of the shed door. Where did they come from? He shut the door, locked it, and retraced his steps. The blue shoeprints led down the brick path, onto the driveway, and then toward the street. At the street, the prints vanished.

Why hadn't Dylan noticed the prints? Probably because he had been rushing to his motorcycle. Max and his older brother were always arguing about which was the better set of wheels: motorcycle or scooter. Max kept a growing list in his head. This morning, he had a new item for his list:

#11. Scooter drivers are more observant.
Motorcyclists miss things.

"Hey, Max!" yelled Lily.

"¡Hola!" said Oscar.

Max looked up and saw his two friends smiling, gliding toward him on their Stingray and Vortex scooters. On Lily's left ear clung a familiar splash of bright apple green. It was Speck, short for Spectrum.

"Why the funny look?" asked Oscar.

Max pointed to the shoeprints.

"Whose are those?" asked Lily, no longer smiling.

Max shook his head. "They weren't there last night."

"They're glowing," said Oscar.

11

"They lead all the way back to the shed," said Max.

"The trunk!" said Lily.

"Don't worry," said Max. "I already looked. It's still there."

Lily and Oscar parked their scooters inside the shed as Max flipped a switch and turned on a dusty, overhead bulb. Speck blinked his tiny eye-cones at the sudden light.

The stiff plastic tarp rustled like wrapping paper as Max pulled it off the trunk. "It looks all right," he said.

"You didn't open it up last night, did you?" asked Lily.

"I gave you my word," said Max.

"How can we open it without a key?" asked Oscar.

"Hammer?" suggested Lily.

"My dad has tools," said Max. "I think."

He and Lily began searching through boxes and shelves.

CREEE-EEEAAAKK!

Like a suitcase sitting on its side, the steamer trunk swung open into two sections.

"But how—?" gasped Lily.

Oscar smiled. "It was unlocked," he said.

The three spies peered into the trunk's dark interior. Speck hopped down from Lily's ear to her shoulder for a better look. One section of the trunk was covered with a blue velvet curtain, the other section held six drawers. A metal plate on the inside said: Let None Disturb My Drawers.

"Think that's a curse?" asked Oscar.

"Well, it's too late now," said Lily.

"Cool, little shelves," said Max. "Let's open one. Hey—!"

As he pulled out a drawer, a white rabbit leaped out and landed in Lily's startled hands. Speck darted to the safety of her ear. Lily's scream turned into a laugh.

"It's fake," said Lily. "Look, Speck." She held the rabbit up and showed a metal spring fastened under its furry stomach. The tiny green chameleon was not amused.

"Who'd keep a bogus bunny in an underwear drawer?" asked Oscar.

"The same guy who'd travel with one of these," said Max, holding out his hand.

"A crystal ball!" whispered Lily.

A globe of pure glass, the size of a baseball, rested in Max's right palm.

"The guy was a wizard," said Max.

"A magician," said Oscar.

Behind the blue velvet curtain they found a magician's clothes. Black tuxedos hung on wooden hangers. Shiny robes of red, black, and gold were folded up neatly on the bottom. On top of the robes sat a silver turban draped with pearls and red gems.

"Do you think they're real?" wondered Max.

"I think everything in this trunk is fake," said Lily.

"Not this," said Oscar. He was examining one of the small drawers. He pulled out a stiff yellowing sheet of paper. They huddled around and read:

AMAZING! INCREDIBLE!

MEMNON THE MAGNIFICENT
World's Greatest Living Magician
Performing Feats of Magic,
Levitation, Prestidigitation,
& Raising Famous Spirits from the Dead

ONLY THREE NIGHTS
at the
HOTEL METROVILLE DELUXE
7:30 P.M.
Closing with a special late-night show
on Halloween

FANTASTIC! SPECTACULAR!

"Never heard of him," said Max.

"He was a long time ago," said Lily. "Is there a date on that, Oscar?"

Oscar squinted at the bottom of the sheet. "1923," he read.

"That's almost a hundred years ago," said Max.

"Do you think he really raised spirits from the dead?" asked Oscar.

Lily shook her head.

"Some magic is real," said Max.

Oscar nodded. "My family celebrates the Day of the Dead. *El Dia de los Muertos.* That's when the spirits of our dead relatives can come back to visit us."

"Have you seen any spirits?" asked Lily.

"No," said Oscar. "But we put out presents for them. Flowers, candy, bread, little skulls of sugar or chocolate. And the next morning, a few presents are missing."

Speck decided that the dark open drawers made a welcome hiding spot. He flashed through the air and landed in a drawer with a soft thud.

"Get back here, Speck," said Lily.

She fished her hand inside the drawer, shuffling more papers. Along with the tiny chameleon, she pulled out a fistful of old newspaper clippings.She noticed the clippings had drawings attached instead of modern-day photos. She froze. One of the drawings was the same weird dog-design that covered the trunk.

"What is it?" said Oscar.

"Listen to this," said Lily. She read, "*Memnon the Magnificent called on the spirits of ancient Egypt to help him raise the dead during his show last night at the Hotel Metroville. His assistants were dressed as Egyptian magicians, with colorful masks in the shape of Anubis."*

"What's a noobis?" asked Max.

"I'm not done," said Lily. She continued, *"Anubis is the jackal-headed god of early Egypt. During an interview with this reporter, Memnon explained that the jackal was considered a guardian of the dead. 'Jackals visit graves,' said Memnon. 'And lead the departed spirits to the underground Land of the Dead.'"*

They were all quiet.

Max cleared his throat. "I forgot to tell you. That dog—"

"The one we heard back at the construction site?" asked Oscar.

"Yeah, I heard it again last night. And so did my brother."

"Did you see it?" asked Lily. Her hands were starting to sweat.

"No," said Max. "But it was late, after midnight."

"Then how do you know it was the same dog?" said Lily. "Maybe it's just some dog in your neighborhood."

"There's only Mrs. Pardo's poodle, Tasha, in this neighborhood," said Max. "At least, that I've ever seen. And I've lived here all my life. Besides, it was the same exact howling. I'd remember that weird noise anywhere."

"You think it was Newbis?" said Oscar.

"Anubis," said Lily. "That's fake stuff. Like the rabbit."

"Then how come we found that trunk right where we were jumping?" asked Max. "How come no one else found it? It's got to be magic. And why did we hear that dog howling right *after* we dug up the trunk?"

Lily didn't have an answer to his questions.

"Let's go ride our scooters by the river," said Lily. "We only have another week before school starts up."

They closed the trunk and hid it once more beneath the green plastic tarp. Outside, the sun peeked through the heavy clouds. Max locked the shed.

Oscar gripped his scooter handlebar, and set his foot on the aluminum floorboard. "You think those blue footprints have something to do with that magician guy?" he asked.

"Maybe it's his dead spirit coming back for his trunk," suggested Max.

Lily wasn't listening. She was bent down in the grass next to her scooter.

"Did you lose Speck?" asked Max.

Lily shook her head. "No, but something else is gone."

The glowing blue footprints had vanished.

3

VISITORS

"Lily! Turn off the computer when it's storming," Sharon Blue called from the living room of their house.

"All right, Mom," Lily yelled from her bedroom. "Speck, get off the paper. I'm trying to write."

Speck sat motionless, blinking at Lily's glowing computer screen. Lily was busily scanning the Net and writing down notes on a yellow pad. Most of her notes concerned Memnon the Magnificent.

Sharon Blue entered Lily's room. She was hooking a heavy flashlight to her work belt. "I'm off to the University, Lily," she said. "Page me if you need anything. And get off the computer."

"I'm almost finished," said Lily.

"I thought you were going over to Max's house."

"I did. But we can't ride scooters in the rain."

Sharon Blue glanced at her watch. "I'm late. I'll call you on my break." Lily's mother worked as a security guard for the University of Metroville. Even during school vacation, she patrolled the

University buildings and parking lots twice a day. "Keep the door locked," Sharon ordered as she walked through the front hall and out the door.

Lily waved to her mother through the window, then returned to her notes.

Memnon the Magnificent, born 1885, died 1923. World-famous magician known for special tricks:

> **The Floating Woman**
> **Calling the Spirits**
> **India Rope-climbing Trick**

Performed throughout U.S., Canada, Europe, and South America.
Home in Florida, built in the shape of ancient Egyptian pyramid.

Lily looked at that last item. "I wonder if he kept hitting his head on the slanty ceilings," she said to Speck. Speck blinked at the funny, wormy squiggles on the yellow paper. He flicked out his tiny tongue, then rolled his eye-cones. Crickets, Speck decided, tasted much better than ink.

Tap, tap.

Lily jumped. A hand was scratching at her bedroom window.

She tiptoed over to the window. It was Oscar. She pointed to her front door and ran into the hallway to let him in.

"I'm not supposed to have anyone over," said Lily.

"Sorry," said Oscar, his hair dripping on her front-hall rug. "Can I park my scooter on your porch?"

Lily nodded. "What's that under your T-shirt?"

Oscar grinned and pulled out a folded-up newspaper.

"I saw this at the store," he said. Oscar worked as a delivery boy for his father's grocery store, Santiago Market. He zoomed all over the University grounds delivering ice on the back of his scooter. The students and teachers nicknamed him Ice Boy.

"My father doesn't let me make deliveries in the rain," said Oscar. "So my brother Carlos and I were cleaning and sweeping up. I was stacking up some old newspapers in the back of the store. This paper's from two days ago."

"What's so special about it?" asked Lily.

Oscar pointed to an article on the lower half of the front page.

ROBBERY AT MOODY MUSEUM

"I've heard of the Moody Museum," said Lily. "It's in the old part of downtown."

"Read what the robbers took," said Oscar.

Lily didn't know why Oscar had such a strange

look in his eyes. Then she saw the name: Memnon the Magnificent.

Lily gasped, "The same Memnon the Magnificent?"

"I doubt if there are two," said Oscar.

The paper stated that the museum had been broken into two days ago. Only one item was stolen: a steamer trunk belonging to the dead magician.

"That's not all," said Oscar. "What's really creepy is that the museum people don't know how the trunk was taken out of the building."

"The crooks probably broke a window," said Lily.

"All the doors were locked from the inside," said Oscar. "And no windows were broken. That's what the paper says."

Lily sank into a chair in the hallway. "Like a magician's trick. So how did the trunk get buried at the construction site?"

Oscar shrugged.

Lily ran to her room and returned with her yellow pad. "Listen to what I found out about Memnon," she said. She read her notes to Oscar. "Remember how I said that steamer trunks were used on ships like the *Titanic*?"

Oscar nodded.

"Well, after Memnon did his show at the Hotel Metroville in 1923, he got on a ship for South America. It was called *The Rose of Peru*. But it got caught in a storm out in the Gulf and it sank!"

"Was his trunk on the ship?" asked Oscar.

"Yes, but it washed ashore after the storm. Some kids back in 1923 found it on the beach."

"Like we found it at the construction site," said Oscar.

"There were no survivors from *The Rose of Peru*," said Lily. "Only the trunk."

Thunder rumbled outside.

"First it escaped from the sinking ship," said Oscar. "Then it escaped from the museum. Maybe next it will escape from Max's shed."

Lily picked up the hall phone. "We need to call the Moody Museum and have them take it away."

"Call Max first," said Oscar. "Let him know what's going on."

As Lily held the phone to her ear and dialed, she stared at the dripping Oscar. She glanced out the window at his scooter drying on the porch. "Why didn't you call me on the phone?" Lily asked. "Instead of getting all wet?"

"My parents won't let me use the phone during a storm," Oscar said.

"What is it with grown-ups and electricity?" wondered Lily.

The phone was ringing at the other end.

"Max isn't answering," Lily said.

The phone rang ten, twelve, thirteen times.

"Where is he?" said Lily.

* * *

Max Martin flipped on the light switch in the shed.

Memnon's trunk still sat under the stiff plastic tarp.

"What I need now," Max said to himself, "is a second hiding place."

He shot a glance through the shed's single window. Good, Dylan's motorcycle was still gone. Soccer practice didn't stop for rain. His dad was still working in his office. Max could see a lamp glowing through the window blinds.

Max needed a second hiding spot for the object he carried in his left hand. It was the one sneaker that escaped from the mud pit last night. Max was worried that if his father saw the sneaker in his room, he might also notice the other one was missing. Max's father taught astronomy at the University of Metroville. He was good at observing small and unexplainable objects. Max didn't want to explain to his father about the mud pit, or the steamer trunk, or flying his scooter off the mountain of dirt. Max did not want to get grounded for life.

The rain stopped hammering on the roof of the shed. Max stared at the steamer trunk. Even with the lightbulb on, the trunk gave Max a weird feeling.

Lily thinks everything in the trunk is fake, thought Max. But the barking dog was real. The footprints were real.

The footprints were also gone. *They must have been paint,* Max thought. The rain had washed them away. But it hadn't started raining while he and his friends were in the shed.

ARRR-OOOOOOOH!

The howl came from outside, just below the shed window. Max looked at the shed door. It was unlocked. Whoever was outside could easily get inside.

Max dashed over to the door of the shed and stumbled over a toolbox. Ouch! The shoe flew out of his hand. Max picked himself up and slammed the door shut.

ARRR-GGGGGH!

Max leaned with his back against the door. Something pushed against it from the other side. A low growl rumbled at the foot of the door.

Max latched the door from the inside and then looked out the window. Dylan's cycle was still gone. The lamp still burned in his dad's office. Why couldn't they have seen him walking toward the shed? Why didn't his dad follow him out here and ask what he was doing? Then he wouldn't be alone with the jackal, or Anubis, or whatever it was.

This would be a great time to have a cell phone, Max thought.

A slobbering, snuffling sound came from the other side of the shed. The creature was circling him. No one would hear Max if he yelled. He didn't want to attract the attention of the dog-thing outside or make it angry. There was a chance it still didn't realize Max was in the shed.

At least he was safe inside.

Max stared at the cement floor. A blue footprint . . . inside the shed.

The outside prints had ended at the door. There hadn't been any prints on the shed floor when Oscar and Lily visited that morning.

Someone else was inside.

But the door was locked. And the dusty window, the only window, was nailed shut.

Max held his breath and glanced swiftly around him. Everything seemed in place. The dusty bulb was not strong enough to light every corner. Shadows lurked under shelves, along roof beams, behind piles of cardboard boxes. Was Oscar right? Could spirits come back as they do on the Day of the Dead?

Max spied a rat on the floor. No, it was his shoe, lying on its side. The sneaker lay a few feet away from the weird blue prints.

ARRR-OOOOOOOH!

The howl sounded farther away. Max glanced out the window again. This time he saw his father peering through the window in his office. His father's nose was pressed against the glass. Neither Max nor his father saw any sign of a dog, with or without pointy ears.

Max bent down to pick up the shoe and then grinned. The underside of his shoe was covered with a thin layer of blue paint. Max looked at the print on the cement floor. Then he looked at the bottom of his shoe again.

His own shoe had made the print.

When he had stumbled over the toolbox and the shoe flew out of his hand, it had hit the floor and made a print. But how did it get the blue paint on it in the first place? He wasn't wearing the shoe that morning when he had discovered the mysterious prints on the brick path. The last time he'd worn it was at the construction site.

The site! He had slipped his shoe off after he and Oscar pulled Lily from the mud. He remembered seeing barrels of paint when he zigzagged down the back of the mountain. He must have stepped in some when he scootered past them. The paint didn't get washed off because he hadn't worn it home. He had tied the sneakers to his Hurricane's handlebars, and the rain couldn't reach the underside of the shoe.

That explained the footprint inside the shed. What about the prints on the brick walk?

Someone else had stepped into the paint at the construction site and followed him home.

Someone who was after the magician's trunk.

The howling had stopped. Max waited five more minutes, then he inched open the shed door. No sign or sound of a dog. The wind rustled through the grass. Gloomy clouds gathered overhead. A few streetlights lit the sidewalk.

"I don't believe it," said Max.

The brick path was covered with a new set of blue prints. Glowing blue pawprints left by some huge unseen hound.

4

MEATBALLS

"That's where the blue paint came from," said Max.

The three spies scootered closer to the mountain of dirt. The construction site was deserted. A pale half-moon gleamed in a sky full of scudding clouds.

"From those barrels," said Max.

Lily braked her black-and-gold Stingray next to a metal barrel. "This one's as tall as me," she said.

"Luminescent paint," read Oscar. "That means it glows."

"Only when light is flashed at it," said Max. "I think they use it for safety barriers in a parking lot. The car beams hit it and the driver can't miss it."

Lily kicked her scooter carefully over the dirt. She bent low over her handlebars, aiming her flashlight at the ground, spying for spilled paint. Her voice echoed against the metal barrels. "You

28

think whoever made those footprints was watching us that night?" she asked.

"I think someone was spying on us," said Max. "They accidentally stepped into the paint, like I did. Then he—or she—"

"Or It," said Oscar.

"—followed us back to the shed," said Max.

"What about the dog?" asked Lily.

Max shrugged. "I haven't figured that out yet."

"There hasn't been any howling," said Oscar.

"Not since that creature trapped me in the shed," said Max.

"I still think we should call the Moody Museum," said Lily.

"First we need time to hunt for clues," said Max. "We'll call them tomorrow, I promise. Then maybe that stupid dog will leave me alone."

"Noobis," said Oscar.

"Ah-nubis," said Lily. "Ah, Ah."

"Aha," said Max. "Look at this."

Oscar and Lily wheeled over to Max's silver Hurricane. He was pointing to a weird tangled mess in the dirt next to a paint barrel.

"Yuck! What is that?" asked Oscar.

"It's just a hair net," said Lily. She bent down and carefully picked it up between her thumb and forefinger. "No big deal."

"No big deal?" said Max.

"Lots of people wear hair nets," she said.

"At a construction site?"

"Maybe some worker got a special hairdo," suggested Lily.

"No construction guy's gonna get a special hairdo," mocked Max.

"Not all construction workers are guys," said Lily.

"Wouldn't you notice if your hair net fell off?" said Oscar.

Max looked at the tangle in Lily's hand. "Who else wears that kind of thing?"

"Hmmm, people at hair salons," said Lily.

"Cooks," said Oscar.

"Cooks?"

"Yeah, to keep their hair out of other people's food," said Oscar. "I've seen my sister Selma wear one when she works at the restaurant."

Lily looked at Max. "Why do you think this is a clue?"

"Because it's odd," said Max. "Anything that doesn't seem to belong here could be a clue."

"Well, that sure is odd over there," she said.

Her flashlight was shining toward the floor of the new parking ramp. A few of the parking levels were almost finished.

"It's just a cement floor," said Max.

"With a very special decoration," said Lily. They scootered closer and saw a glowing blue line streaming across the ramp floor.

"A bicycle tire," said Oscar.

Lily nodded. "Someone rode their bike across that same paint. And I'll bet it wasn't a worker."

"And the parking level above kept the rain from washing it away," said Max.

"The workers wouldn't notice it during the day," added Oscar.

"Let's follow it," said Lily.

She led them whizzing across the ramp and out of the construction site. Her flashlight picked out a few disconnected streaks of blue along sidewalks and streets.

"The rain washed most of it away," said Lily. "But there's enough to follow."

Max steered his Hurricane next to the Stingray. "The bike tires stamped the paint into the ground harder than those shoeprints we saw."

"What's that smell?" asked Oscar. *Delicioso.*

Lily sniffed. "You're right. Yummy."

The faint, glowing blue line had led to an older part of Metroville. Narrow streets were full of parked cars. Bright, cheerful restaurants and coffee shops sat on every corner.

The three scooters glided down a dim alley. The back door of a restaurant stood open. Light and rock music poured out. "The line ends here," said Lily, clicking off her flashlight.

"It's pizza," said Max.

"Spaghetti," said Oscar.

"Meatballs," Lily said. "Roasted garlic meatballs with Portobello mushrooms."

Max and Oscar both stared at her. "How the heck do you know that?" said Max.

Lily smiled. "I've been here before with my mom. This is one of her favorite places to eat. And that's what she always orders."

A large shadow filled the open doorway.

"What are you kids doing back here?"

A large man with huge, muscular arms stood before them in a sleeveless T-shirt. A vast white apron covered his waist. "You trying to sneak in?"

Max shook his head. "No, honest. We were just driving through here."

The man set his huge fists on his hips. "I don't need you messing up my trash cans again."

"What do you mean?" said Oscar. "We've never been back here before."

"Then who's been making a mess back here every night?" said the huge man. "Get out of here! Go on!"

The scooter spies darted quickly to the end of the alley. The huge man watched them go and then walked slowly back into the restaurant.

On the sidewalk in front of the restaurant, the three spies skidded to a stop.

"Did you see what I saw back there?" said Max, triumphantly.

"Where?" said Lily.

"On that big guy's head," said Max. "He was wearing a hair net."

"So, what do we do now?" asked Lily. "Follow him home? Ask him about steamer trunks and magicians?"

"Just because the blue bike tires ended here, doesn't mean that guy was the one spying on us," said Oscar. "This place must have more than one cook. And maybe different ones on different nights."

"We need more clues," said Max.

"Let's go back to the alley," said Lily. "But let's go the long way around."

They zipped along the sidewalk and turned sharply at the corner. The scooters glided past the alley's entrance. As they flew over a dark, deserted street, they heard a familiar sound.

ARRR-OOOOOOOH!

"Forget the alley," said Oscar.

Lily saw a dark, galloping shape following them on the sidewalk.

"Hurry!" said Lily.

They raced along the narrow streets, flew past gloomy apartment buildings, and rocketed through empty bus stands.

"I think it's getting closer," yelled Max. He heard a low growl at his back.

A flash of light blinded the spies. A large white Jeep full of laughing students and loud blaring dance music cruised past them. The Hurricane, Vortex, and Stingray ground to a stop.

"It's gone," said Oscar, looking behind them.

"The light must have scared it," said Lily.

"Yeah, like it scares vampires," muttered Max.

Lily looked up at the crisp, half-moon. Then she looked at the empty sidewalk behind them. "Tomorrow, we are calling that museum," she said.

5

MOODY AND STERN

The doorbell buzzed at the Martin house.

"Hello, Mr. Martin? I'm Dr. Moody."

A tall woman with a wide face and wide smile extended her hand to Max's father. Light poured through the doorway into the early evening air. The light bounced off the bald head of a small man standing at the woman's side. "And this is Dr. Stern," she said. The bald man stared up at Mr. Martin through thick, black-rimmed glasses.

"Charmed," croaked Dr. Stern.

Flashbulbs popped in Mr. Martin's startled face.

"And this is the press," said Dr. Moody. "They are naturally very interested in the discovery of the stolen trunk."

"Naturally," whispered Max to his friends. He stood with his arms crossed, next to Lily and Oscar. The three friends were crowded in the hall next to Max's father.

"Please, come inside," said Mr. Martin.

More cameras flashed as the front door closed.

Mr. Martin led his guests into the living room.

"I can't tell you how thrilled we were to get your phone call," Dr. Moody said, sitting down in a stuffed chair. "This is the first robbery we've ever had at our museum."

"The first," echoed Dr. Stern.

The tall woman smiled. "We're not prepared for this kind of thing. We called the police, of course, but we never dreamed that we would see the Memnon trunk again."

"Never dreamed," added Dr. Stern, frowning at the three young friends.

Dr. Moody turned her wide smile to Max. "So, you're the ones who recovered the trunk."

"Uncovered," said Lily. "It was buried."

Dr. Moody blinked. She looked at Mr. Martin for an explanation. "Buried? I don't understand."

Mr. Martin looked gravely at Max. "My son and his friends were out . . . uh, riding their scooters a few days ago, and they came across the trunk. It seems to have been buried where the new parking ramp is being built downtown. When they told me about it, just this afternoon, we thought we better call you."

Dr. Stern removed his glasses and wiped them with his tie. "When you say construction site, do you mean the site by the old police station?" he croaked.

Lily nodded. "Yes, that's right."

The two doctors exchanged a worried look.

"Is there something wrong?" asked Mr. Martin.

Dr. Stern replaced his glasses. "I'm sure you're too young to remember, Mr. Martin. But Memnon the Magnificent once performed his magic show here in Metroville."

"We read that somewhere," said Lily.

Dr. Moody beamed. "Isn't that marvelous? Metroville was the site of one of his greatest tricks," she said.

"The Return from the Dead," said Dr. Stern.

"And the building where Memnon the Magnificent performed," Dr. Moody went on, "was in the same spot where the new parking ramp is being built."

Max got goosebumps on the back of his neck. "What was the Return from the Dead trick?"

Lily asked, "Did the magician . . . bury himself alive?"

Dr. Moody's eyes sparkled. "What a bright young woman. Yes, he did. And then, after three days, he magically appeared back onstage."

"Did the audience have to sit there the whole time?" asked Max.

Dr. Moody laughed. "No, no. They had tickets to come back three days later."

Max turned to Oscar and whispered, "That trunk was buried in the same place."

Mr. Martin nervously folded and unfolded his

arms. "That's, uh, very interesting," he said. "Well, did you want to take your trunk? I have it in my shed."

Dr. Moody flashed her wide smile again. "We'll just put it in our van. And I'm sure the press will want to speak with you children about your amazing discovery."

"We can't thank you enough," croaked Dr. Stern.

Oscar and Max peered through the front window's curtains at the mob of reporters camped on the lawn. "I think that's the guy from Channel Thirteen," said Oscar.

"I have a question," said Lily. "Is that a jackal on the trunk?"

"The gold design you mean?" said the doctor. "Well, yes and no. Ancient Egyptians drew pictures of animals like those in their temples and tombs. And scientists used to think they were jackals. But in the last few years we've learned that they're really drawings of dogs."

"Dogs?" said Oscar, turning from the window.

Dr. Moody nodded. "Temple dogs. They were trained to guard the tombs of newly buried bodies."

Max remembered the low growl that circled the shed yesterday.

"Thank you again," said Dr. Moody, getting up from her chair. "I can't wait to tell the newspeople that we've recovered the missing trunk. I mean, that *you* recovered it for us. Think of it. Memnon's trunk was found on the third day you kids were at the construction site, just as Memnon reappeared after three days."

"Three days," said Dr. Stern.

"Do you think he was a good magician?" asked Lily.

"Indeed," said Dr. Moody, cheerfully. "One of the greatest. Like Houdini. Or David Copperfield."

"We can get outside through this side door," said Mr. Martin.

"And for finding the trunk, you'll all be granted lifetime passes to the museum," said the tall Dr. Moody.

Mr. Martin took Max aside before he led the doctors outside. "I want you kids to stay in here. It's a good thing you were able to help out the museum. But I don't ever want to catch you, or hear about you, hanging around that site again. Understand? It's dangerous."

Max and his friends watched the two doctors follow his dad to the shed. Dr. Moody posed for photographers as Dr. Stern and Mr. Martin carried the trunk to the front yard.

Lily turned away from the window. "I think something funny is going on."

"You don't believe the trunk magically disappeared and reappeared?" asked Max.

"Did you hear what Dr. Moody said to me?" said Lily.

"That jackals are really dogs," said Oscar.

"Not that," said Lily. "She said it was weird that we found the trunk after visiting the site for three days. Three days."

"Like Memnon's magic trick," added Max.

"Right," said Lily. "But I never said we were there three days. Did you?"

Oscar and Max both looked grim. Max said slowly, "My dad didn't say that, either."

"So how did Dr. Smiley know that?" Lily asked.

* * *

The Moody Museum's white walls gleamed like bones in the moonlight.

"If my dad learns we came here on just our scooters," said Max, "he's gonna kill me."

ARRR-OOOOOOOH!

Three sets of wheels suddenly braked.

"It's that same dog!" cried Max.

"It's behind the museum," said Oscar. The three spies kicked off and rocketed toward the back of the huge, dark building.

"Someone's running down the alley!" shouted Oscar.

His gleaming electric-blue Vortex Racer pulled ahead of Max and Lily's scooters. He whizzed past loading docks built into the side of the old museum. At the back, the alley narrowed. The alley sloped upward to the second floor of the museum, leveled off, then slanted back down to the other side.

"I see him up there," cried Lily. She tightened her grip on the Stingray's handlebars. It took extra kicks to reach the top of the alley. All three scooters skidded noisily to a stop.

"Where is he?" demanded Max.

The alley was full of thick shadows. In the humid night air, the stars were fogged over. Dim light came from old-fashioned streetlamps standing at each end of the alley.

"I don't hear anything," said Lily. "But I was sure I saw someone running back here."

They were startled by a new light. One of the windows in the museum lit up. Two shadows moved against the window's shade.

"The doctors," said Max. The three spies glided toward the window.

"*ARRR-OOOOOOOH!*

"It's down the other side," said Max.

Lily turned and said, "You two follow that dog or whatever it is. I'll stay here."

Oscar nodded. "We'll be right back," he promised.

The two boys each made a running push and a leap onto the decks of their scooters. The

41

Hurricane and the Vortex flew down the alley's ramp like twin comets and disappeared into the darkness.

Lily watched them vanish and then turned back toward the window. She heard loud, excited voices.

"By tomorrow night," said Dr. Moody, "we'll be in all the papers and on all the nightly news."

Lily heard a funny smack. Was Dr. Stern rubbing his greedy hands together?

"Delightful! Delightful!" he crowed. "And Moody's Museum will be full of customers. People who will pay to stare at the disappearing magic trunk. It will be like the old days."

"And to think we had that old trunk in the museum basement all these years," said Dr. Moody. "If I hadn't been organizing down there . . . I hope the press doesn't ask too many more questions," she muttered.

"And what if they do?" said the little doctor. "They'll never learn that it was you and I who buried that trunk in the construction site. We're lucky I spied those kids playing there. I knew it was only a matter of time before they found it."

"I was worried the construction workers would find it," said Dr. Moody.

"Not with me watching that site from my parked car for three days and nights," said Dr. Stern. "And if that boy's father hadn't called us, we could have pretended that we got an anonymous phonecall. One way or other, we'd still end up with the trunk and the publicity."

"I guess you're right," said Dr. Moody. "It all worked out."

Lucy was puzzled. The doctors had known that the trunk was in Max's shed all the time. So who had made the glowing blue prints? Dr. Stern drove a car, not a bicycle. Was there *another* spy in the construction site?

And where had the jackal-dog come from?

6

THE SHADOW OF ANUBIS

Oscar and Max tore through the dark alleys and streets behind the Moody Museum like bloodhounds on wheels. Each time they reached a new street corner, the unseen dog's bark would lead them down another alley.

"That dog must be on a scooter himself," Max muttered.

The two spies flew over deserted sidewalks, skimmed along empty streets, sailed past endless lines of parked cars. Oscar had never been in this section of Metroville before. It was far from the University and the Mixaloopi River.

"*ARRR-OOOOOOOH!*

Max yelled, "He ducked into that alley behind the closed pizza shop. Over there!"

The scooters veered between tall, gloomy buildings. A dark, lumpy figure was gliding far ahead of them.

"I was right," said Max."He's on wheels."

As the figure raced beneath a streetlight, Max

and Oscar finally got a glimpse of their quarry. A young man was swooping along on a bicycle. A dark doglike shadow raced at his side.

"So that's Anubis," thought Oscar.

The man steered the bike gracefully around garbage cans and fire hydrants. He hopped on and off curbs without losing speed. The shadow never left his side.

Max added another item to his mental list:

#12. Scooters can go anywhere bikes can go.

On a dingy sidewalk, the biker aimed toward a homemade ramp that some skateboarders had left out. The bike soared up the ramp, flew three feet into the air, and landed on the other side of a metal fence.

The Hurricane and the Vortex squealed to a stop. Max revised his list by adding the word 'almost' to the latest item.

Oscar pounded on his handlebars. "Who is that guy?" he asked.

Max was winded "I think . . . he's the guy . . . from the restaurant . . ."

"The hairnet guy?" said Oscar.

Max nodded. "The guy . . . who stepped in . . . the paint."

* * *

Lily heard scooter tires skidding to a stop behind her.

"We lost him," Oscar said, breathlessly.

"Anubis?" asked Lily.

"Looks more like a black lab or German shepherd," said Max. "We chased them all over town."

"Do you think that's the guy from the restaurant?" asked Lily.

The boys nodded. She filled in Max and Oscar on the rest of the doctors' conversation.

"I thought it was strange finding a trunk right where we landed the scooters," said Oscar.

"That's how Dr. Moody knew we'd been there for three days," said Lily. "The doctors had picked out the construction site for their publicity stunt. Then we came along. They spied on us for three nights."

"So, our scooter flying gave them the idea to bury the trunk at the bottom of the dirt mountain," said Max.

"Did you ever get the feeling we were being watched those nights?" asked Oscar.

"Yeah," said Max. "But I didn't say anything. I thought it was just a dumb feeling."

Lily turned back to the window. She looked quickly to her right and left. "I don't see any open windows back here," she said. "We need to get in there and find out what else is going on."

"The truck dock," suggested Max.

The three spies scootered down the alley's ramp and pulled into the dark and deserted truck dock. A wide ledge ran alongside the museum. Up a short flight of cement steps, the spies reached the ledge. Two large metal doors faced them.

"This is where trucks drop off shipments for the museum," said Max.

"Like haunted steamer trunks," grinned Oscar.

"Those big doors are too heavy to lift," said Lily.

Max winked. "The doors aren't always shut all the way." He led them over to the second metal door. Half-hidden in the dark, the door did not reach all the way to the ledge's floor.

"How did you know this door was open?" asked Oscar.

Max smiled. "Let's just say, I like riding my scooter a lot at night." Max remembered one of the first notes he ever made to his mental list:

#13. Scooters are quieter than motorcycles and better for spying out the city.

"So we have to crawl under that?" asked Lily.

"Unless you want to knock at the front door," said Max.

Lily made a face, pushed her scooter sideways through the gap in the doorway, and then slid inside after it.

Max and Oscar followed her. "Motorcycles

can't squeeze through twelve inches, either," said Max.

"What did you say?" asked Oscar.

"Oh, uh, nothing."

"Quiet!" Lily shushed them. The inner truck dock was darker than outside. The only light filtered in through the bottom of the metal door. Lily led them up a flight of steps and through a door. They found themselves in a side hallway of the museum.

"I hear voices," whispered Oscar.

The three spies crept into the main gallery of the Moody Museum. They silently wheeled their scooters behind one of the huge three-story pillars.

Oscar pointed soundlessly toward the steamer trunk. It sat on a low wooden pedestal. Dr. Moody and Dr. Stern stood next to the trunk. Dr. Moody was buttoning her coat.

"ARRR-OOOOOOOH!"

"There's that blasted howl again outside," said Dr. Stern. "It's getting on my nerves."

"It's just a dog," said the tall Dr. Moody. Then she chuckled. "Or the curse of Memnon the Magnificent," she added.

The doctors began walking toward a side door.

"Tomorrow is an even bigger day," Dr. Stern croaked. "That's when Memnon's spirit returns to the construction site."

The three spies looked at each other.

Dr. Moody looked anxious. "I hope you know what you're doing."

"Tut, tut," croaked the bald, little doctor. In his hand he held out the crystal ball that Max had found in the trunk. "Tomorrow the reporters will watch me reenact the discovery of the trunk," he said . "I'll stand with a shovel in my hands by that dirt mountain. Then I'll dig a little bit. When this ball comes out of the dirt, that will give them something more to write about. And new visitors will pour into our museum!"

"It will make a marvelous photo," said Dr. Moody.

"It will make us a lot of money," said Dr. Stern with a chuckle.

A second before he shut the door behind him, Dr. Stern reached out a bony finger. He pressed a red button on the wall. Then he slammed the door shut.

The three spies had been crouching behind a pillar. Max suddenly lifted his head. "What's that grinding sound?"

"Look at the front door!" screamed Lily.

A metal gate was sliding out of the wall and sealing off the front door. The main gallery of the museum echoed with the groans and screams of metal gates sliding into place.

"The side door, too!" yelled Oscar.

The spies mounted their scooters and raced back

to the door that led from the truck dock. Too late. A heavy metal gate blocked their way. All the lights were blinking off, one by one. Only a few red worklights remained glowing.

"Let's get back to the trunk," shouted Lily.

The scooters slid across the marble floor. As they braked near the dead magician's trunk, metal gates slid in front of the pillars. The gallery was being barricaded with dozens of thick metal bars. Max felt like an animal at the zoo.

Silence. The metal gates stopped moving.

"Trapped," moaned Lily.

"With Anubis," said Oscar, looking grimly at the silent steamer trunk.

7

THE INDIA ROPE-CLIMBING TRICK

"What do we do now?" Lily asked with a groan.

"We need to get out of here," said Oscar, looking up at the metal gates surrounding them.

"There are no crossbars to climb up," said Max. "The bars are flat. We can't scoot up them without ripping open our legs. And that gate is at least fifteen feet high."

Lily gripped two of the bars and stared across the main gallery of the museum.

"There's an elevator over there," she said. "I'll bet it goes up to the doctors' office."

"Big deal," said Max. "We can't get over there. And if we did, how can we get down from a second- or third-story window? Fly?"

Lily spun around and faced him. "Don't you remember? The alley is higher behind the building. The window we saw back there is actually on the second floor."

Oscar hopped up off the floor where he'd been sitting. "You're right! We could just open the window and climb out. Who cares if it sets off an alarm. We'll be long gone on our scooters by then."

"Okay, Mr. and Mrs. Houdini, how do we pass through the bars and reach the elevator?" grumbled Max. He walked over and sat on the magician's steamer trunk with a sigh. Then he gazed down at the trunk. "Too bad Memnon isn't around to help us with a magic trick," he murmured.

Oscar sat down next to him. "If Memnon could raise the dead, maybe he could raise the living and lift us over those bars."

"Maybe he can" said Lily, with a gleam in her eyes.

Max groaned. "You don't believe in magic and Anubis and stuff, do you?"

"I believe in tricks," said Lily. "And that trunk is full of them."

The spies threw open the steamer trunk. They yanked out all the drawers, opened every box and container, unzipped every secret compartment. The bogus bunny surprised them again. Lily found an old brochure from one of Memnon's bad-luck cruises. In the dim red glow of the worklights she read the words printed across the front: *The Rose of Peru*. It was the ship that sailed for South America and had hit the powerful storm in the Gulf of Mexico.

Oscar found a magic wand, a top hat, a deck of

cards, a cage with two fake doves inside, and a second crystal ball. He also found a gold statue of the pointy-eared dog, Anubis. But nothing that would help them escape from the museum.

"Ah!" exclaimed Max. From under the folded robes on the bottom of the trunk, he pulled a long coil of rope.

"That's from his India Rope-climbing Trick," said Lily. She had seen the trick's name during her computer search for the magician.

"I hope we don't have to be in India for the trick to work," said Oscar.

"Not this trick," said Max. He held the rope loosely in his hands. Then he tossed one end of the coil up and over the top of the metal gate.

"¡Estupendo!" said Oscar. "Just like the rodeo."

One end of the rope dangled a few inches beyond the metal gate. Lily reached through the bars and grabbed it. "Hold that end of the rope," said Max. Oscar and Lily grasped the rope and braced their feet against the floor. Max spit on his hands, grabbed his half of the rope, and pulled, bracing his feet against the metal bars. The rope instantly snapped in half.

"It's fake, too!" said Lily.

"There has to be something," said Max.

"What about the robes?" asked Oscar.

Lily rolled her eyes. "We're gonna get dressed up?"

"Tie the robes together," said Oscar. "Make a rope out of them."

Each magician robe was six-feet long. Tied together, the strong fabric made a "rope" that stretched sixteen feet.

"*Estupendo*," said Max.

Oscar tossed the end of the homemade rope over the gate. Each end dangled seven feet off the ground. "Push the trunk over here," said Oscar. They set the steamer trunk against the gate. Oscar climbed on top of the steamer trunk and grasped both ends of the tied cloaks. He climbed the gate like a lineman climbing a telephone pole. Balancing himself at the top of the gate, he tied one end of the robe-rope to the top rail. He swung his legs over the side, grabbed the rope, which now hung all the way to the floor, and clambered down into the gallery.

"It's easy," said Oscar.

Lily climbed like a spider monkey to the top of the gate and down into the gallery.

Before Max climbed to freedom, he passed the three scooters between the metal bars. "Don't forget these," he said. Max made another note to himself.

#14. Scooters can do escape tricks.

If Houdini were still alive, Max thought, he'd ride a scooter instead of a motorcycle.

When all three spies were together in the gallery, Oscar flicked the end of the robe-rope. The knot on the top rail came loose. The bright rope collapsed into Oscar's hands.

"Slip knot," he grinned. "We might need this rope somewhere else."

On the opposite side of the gallery, the path to the elevators was clear. In less than five minutes, the spies and their scooters were inside the elevator rising to the second floor.

Dim red worklights lit their way along a second-floor hall. Lily saw a glass door. They read "Dr. Ernestine Moody, Curator."

"What's a curator?" asked Max.

"Someone who cures you," guessed Lily. "She's a doctor, right?"

The door was unlocked.

"Yow!" Oscar and Lily screamed.

"It's only a skeleton," said Lily.

"So why did you yell, too?" asked Max with a grin.

A plastic skeleton hung from a metal stand in the corner. It reminded Oscar of the costumes his uncles sometimes wore for the Day of the Dead. Lily ignored Max and led them to the window in the back. Just as they thought, the window opened onto the alley.

"The window's already open," said Lily, peeking out.

She screamed. A black shadow leaped through the opening and thudded onto the floor in front of them.

"ARRR-OOOOOOOH!"

They were alone in the dark office with the ghost dog.

8

PHANTOM

The black dog lunged toward them.

"Look out!" yelled Oscar.

The dog flew past the three spies and ran to the office door. A young man with a red goatee stood in the doorway. "I think he's after me," said the man.

The dog nuzzled the man's legs. His huge, wet nose sniffed at the man's feet and hands. The man pulled a plastic bag out of his pocket. He reached inside the bag and pulled out a small round object. The dog barked cheerfully.

"Roasted garlic meatballs with Portobello mushrooms!" cried Lily.

The dog devoured the treat and sniffed for a second helping. The young man stared at Lily. "You're a better detective than I am," he said. "How did you know that?"

"We followed your trail to the restaurant," she said.

"Your bike tires got paint on them from the construction site," said Max.

Oscar watched the shadowy black dog make two more meatballs disappear. "Is he always that hungry?" he asked.

"He is for these," said the man. "He's always following me around. Ever since I caught him behind the restaurant rustling through the trash cans."

"Did you follow us back to my shed?" asked Max.

The man nodded. "I had to keep track of that trunk. Especially since I've been looking for it for so long."

"This is your trunk?" asked Lily.

"My grandfather found it," said the man. "Years ago, when he was a kid, he and his cousins saw it wash up on the beach."

"I read about that on the computer," said Lily.

"Memnon the Magnificent was my grandfather's hero," said the man. "And when the three cousins found the trunk, they decided my grandfather could keep it. The newspapers wrote up the story. Memnon had no living relatives, so legally it belonged to my grandfather."

"How did it end up in the museum?" asked Oscar.

The young man sat down on the office desk. The black dog lay at his feet. "A man named Moody read about it in the papers," said the young man. "He offered to pay my grandfather for it. Said he was a collector. My grandfather refused. Then, one

58

night, the trunk disappeared from my grandfather's house. He always suspected Moody, but he had no way to prove it."

"And now you have proof," said Max.

"I never connected the name Moody with this museum. Not until I read the Metroville paper a few days ago about the trunk and its so-called disappearance. I came over here to see if I could talk with the museum owners. That's when I saw Dr. Stern driving away. I followed him, thinking he was just going home. Instead, he drove over to the construction site and buried the trunk."

"So you were spying on him when he was spying on us," said Max.

"Why didn't you just dig it up yourself?" asked Lily.

Derek shook his head. "I couldn't. Someone was always there. Either the construction workers, or you, or the doctor."

"We need to catch Dr. Stern in the act," said Oscar. "He's gone back to the construction site to plant another magic trick."

Lily had grown bold enough to pet the black dog. His huge pink tongue licked her hands. "Sorry," she said. "No meatballs here."

"Maybe that's why he circled your shed," said Oscar to Max. "He smelled the meatballs from, uh—"

"The name's Derek," said the man.

"What's *his* name?" asked Lily, kneeling next to the hound.

"Don't know," said the man. "He just appeared one night in the alley."

"Not Anubis," said Lily.

"How about A-newer-bis?" joked Max.

"Phantom," suggested Oscar.

Derek nodded. "That's a great name."

"Hey, you dropped that," pointed Max. Derek bent over and picked up a tangle from the office floor. It was a hair net.

"I keep losing these," said Derek. "It must have fallen out of my pocket when I pulled out the meatballs."

"We need to get to the construction site," said Oscar. "And catch that doctor planting the crystal ball."

They all climbed out the window, including Phantom, and began mounting their scooters and bike.

"Max, what's wrong?" asked Oscar.

Max stood like a statue. One foot rested on the Hurricane's deck, the other was planted on the ground. He stared at his handlebars.

"What's wrong?" Oscar repeated.

Max shrugged. "I was just thinking about what my dad told me about not going to the construction site again."

"But we have to," said Lily. "We need to catch

the doctor in the act. Your dad would understand that." She looked at Derek. "Besides, we're going with adult supervision."

Derek grinned. "We better hurry," he said, putting a foot on his bike pedal. "We still might be able to catch the doctor if we take a shortcut across town. Follow me."

* * *

DOOO-OOOO-OOOOOM!
Thunder rumbled over Metroville. Derek was familiar with the streets around the Moody Museum. He led the spies and Phantom through the maze of twisting alleys and narrow sidewalks. They swooped under train bridges, bounced over railroad tracks, and rocketed through small, gloomy parks.

"There's the site!"cried Lily.

Bright worklights surrounding the construction site flickered off and on. "Power must be out over half the city," said Oscar.

Max led the scooters to the front gate of the site. They ducked under the hanging chain as their scooters rushed underneath.

"I don't see the doctor," said Lily.

"Spread out!" shouted Max. "We have to find him if he's still here."

The three scooters, the bike, and the dog raced

off in different directions. Oscar steered toward the parked trucks and heavy machinery. Lily zigged and zagged around piles of concrete blocks and metal pipes. Max kicked his Hurricane toward the mountain of dirt in the middle of the site. Even after the heavy rains of the past two days, the dirt towered high above the ground.

"ARRR-OOOOOOOH!"

"Where's Phantom?" yelled Max.

"He's over by the mountain," said Oscar.

Lily saw the little doctor appearing from behind the dirt mountain carrying a shovel.

The three scooters raced to the base of the mountain. Derek's bicycle zipped out of the dark to join them.

"We know what you're doing," said Lily, confronting Dr. Stern. "It's all fake. Like that phony magician."

"No one will listen to a bunch of brats," croaked Dr. Stern. "This is something you kids don't understand."

"They'll listen to me," said Derek, stepping forward.

"And just who are you supposed to be?" asked the doctor.

"His grandfather found the trunk," said Oscar. "It belongs to him."

"It belongs to the Moody Museum," snarled the doctor.

"Mr. Moody stole it," said Max.

"Prove it," said Dr. Stern.

Lightning flashed over the site. "I wasn't able to prove it before today," said Derek. "But now that I know where the trunk is, I can. My grandfather told me that he practiced card tricks when he was a kid. He kept his deck of cards in Memnon's trunk. And it has his name written on the box."

"I saw that deck," said Oscar.

Dr. Stern goggled through his thick glasses at Derek and Phantom. "You put that deck in there yourself," said the doctor. "You planted it there!"

"How could he?" said Lily. "The trunk has always been in the museum."

"Or else you were spying on it," added Oscar.

"Or it was locked in my shed or inside the museum again," said Max.

"Even when I crawled through the museum window to try and find it, I couldn't get over the metal gates," said Derek.

"So you were inside the museum!" said the doctor.

"But so were we," said Lily. "And he was nowhere near the trunk. We're witnesses."

Thunder rumbled and shook the dirt mountain.

"That doesn't matter now," said Dr. Stern. "You children leave this site. This is a matter for adults."

"*ARRR-OOOOOOOH!*"

63

A roar surrounded the construction site. Rain poured as if a giant faucet had been turned on in the sky.

"Oh, no!" said Lily. The wet ground sucked at her sneakers. "It's happening again!"

The mountain was turning into a monstrous pile of mud. Above them, a dark wall of dirt slowly slid down the mountain's side.

"I'm not going to lose another shoe." said Max.

"Look out, Dr. Stern!" shouted Lily. Her cries were covered by Phantom's growls. The dog leaped at the doctor. The doctor screamed.

"Phantom's trying to save him," said Lily.

GLOOP!

The wall of sliding mud pounded into the landing site. Muck splashed on the faces and arms of the three spies.

"Where's the doctor?" yelled Max.

"Where's Phantom?" said Lily.

Oscar threw himself into the mound of muck that covered the landing site. He closed his eyes and dug into the mud as if he were swimming through peanut butter. Max and Lily each waded in to join him. Lily sank up to her chin in the muck.

"I can feel something with my foot!" she cried. "Ouch! Something tried to bite me. I hope it was Phantom."

Derek ripped off his wristwatch, stuffed it into

his pants pocket, and plunged into the mud along with the three friends.

Oscar's lungs burned. He was afraid of opening his mouth and sucking in mud. He pushed his fingers deeper and deeper into the thick ooze.

Derek burst out of the mud and gasped for air. "I have him!" he cried. With his right arm he yanked a figure from the mud beside him. It was Dr. Stern, bubbling and sputtering for air. Lily thought he looked like an unhappy toad.

"Where's Phantom?" Derek rasped.

The rain kept shoving more mud from the mountain into the landing site.

Oscar felt a thick round shape. He grabbed it, and with a strong kick propelled himself upward out of the mud. He was holding Phantom by a front paw. Max popped up from the mud a second later. He was holding Phantom's tail.

"I got him! I got him!" yelled Max. His pale blond hair was plastered with dark mud.

Oscar laughed. Lily was crying with relief. Phantom began licking her muddy face.

"This would make a great photo for Dr. Moody," joked Oscar.

"Hey, I found something else," Lily said. She threw a muddy lump at Max.

"My shoe!" he cried. Then he added, "But I think I just lost my other one."

9

RETURN OF ANUBIS

A thousand camera bulbs flashed like lightning. Photographers and news reporters surrounded the dirt mountain at the construction site.

"I've never seen what this place looks like in the morning before," said Max.

Max's father draped his arm proudly around his son's shoulders. The reporters kept asking Max and Oscar and Lily questions about their rescue of Dr. Stern last night. Derek was surrounded by a second group of reporters explaining the true history of the magician's trunk. He held Phantom by a brand new leash. The hound was kept quiet with a steady supply of meatballs.

"There it comes," cried Lily. The crowd turned to see the museum van roll slowly through the gates of the construction site. Police officers unhooked the chain at the gate and waved the van through.

"I sure hope that card deck is still there," said Oscar.

"It will be," Lily smiled.

The van rolled to a stop near the dirt mountain. As the van door opened, the photographers clicked their cameras. Dr. Moody did not seem happy with the publicity. Dr. Stern grumbled and kept his head down. Lily's mother, Sharon Blue, wearing her security uniform, stepped out of the back of the van. She opened the two back doors, revealing the magician's steamer trunk.

Reporters pounded the two doctors with questions.

"Is it true you faked the trunk's disappearance?"

"Did old Mr. Moody really steal the trunk?"

"Did you bury that trunk yourself?"

Derek walked over to the trunk. Phantom followed him closely, nuzzling at his knees.

Lily, Oscar, and Max helped lift the trunk onto the ground. Oscar opened it. The blue velvet curtain sparkled in the morning light.

Derek fished through the small drawers. The bogus bunny popped out, scaring a few reporters.

"That dumb bunny will be on TV," Oscar whispered to Max.

"Ah, here it is," said Derek. He lifted up his hand, holding the ancient card deck. He turned the box toward the cameras. Lily could see a name written across the box.

"This proves it," said Derek. "This trunk was discovered by my grandfather over seventy years ago. And since Memnon the Magnificent had no surviving relatives, the trunk rightfully belongs to me."

Dr. Moody and Dr. Stern had both crawled into the van again. They sat glumly in the front seats, their faces turned away from the prying reporters.

"What will happen to the doctors?" asked Lily.

"Jail time," said Max.

"Nah," said Oscar. "All they'll get is a lot of really bad publicity."

"And a strong warning from the cops," added Max.

"ARRR-OOOOOOOH!"

"What is it, Phantom?" asked Lily.

The dog had stopped nuzzling Derek and was now sniffing at one of the trunk's drawers. Lily pulled it open. Inside was a top hat, a pair of fake doves, and a magic wand. Each time she pulled out an object, she was captured on film.

"This is really neat," said Lily. She pulled out the gold statue of the pointy-eared Anubis. The ears of the Egyptian god flashed so brightly in the sunlight, Lily had to shield her eyes. "For hanging around dead people, he sure is pretty," said Lily.

"Can I quote you on that?" asked a reporter.

"Uh, sure," she said.

Lily handed the gold dog to Derek. "This belongs to you, too," she said.

Derek smiled. "Too bad this isn't real gold," he said.

"ARRR-OOOOOOOH!"

As Derek took the statue from Lily, her fingers caught on the dog's tail. There was a loud click. The head of Anubis fell open, swinging on a hinge at the neck.

Derek looked puzzled. He reached inside and pulled out a bulky envelope tied with string.

Max turned to Oscar. "Maybe that's where Memnon kept his extra-dirty underwear."

Derek untied the parcel. His face went white.

Lily took the envelope from him and read the writing across the front of it. "Earnings from Hotel Metroville performance." The envelope was packed with twenty-dollar bills, too many to count all at once!

"It's Memnon's show money," she gasped.

The reporters and photographers grew loud with excitement.

"This is amazing!" said Derek, holding the envelope.

Lily walked over to Max and Oscar.

"That's the real treasure," she said. "I guess part of Memnon did return from the dead."

"How do you think Phantom knew that was in there?" wondered Oscar aloud.

"Maybe he heard Anubis barking," said Lily.

"Dogs can tell when other dogs are around," said Max.

Oscar gazed at the cheerful black dog. Phantom only smiled and wagged his tail.